Fort River School Library
70 South East Street
Amherst, MA 01002

Coconut Crab

by Alex Giannini

Consultant: Darin Collins, DVM
Director, Animal Health Programs
Woodland Park Zoo
Seattle, Washington

New York, New York

Credits

Cover, © Wil Meinderts/Buiten-beeld/Minden; TOC, © Blickwinkel/Alamy; 4–5, © Wil Meinderts/Buiten-beeld/Minden; 6L, © Deep OV/Shutterstock; 6–7, © Carles Zamorano Cabello/Alamy; 8, © satit sewtiw/Shutterstock; 9, © Janos/iStock; 10T, © chameleonseye/iStock; 10B, © Janos Rautonen/Shutterstock; 11, © David Fleetham/Alamy; 12–13, © mkfardlie/Shutterstock; 14L, © Jean-Paul Ferrero/Minden; 14R, © Glenys and Chris/flickr; 15, © Pakhnyushchy/Shutterstock; 16–17, © Jeremy Jowell Africapictures.net/Newscom; 18, © Stephen Belcher/Minden; 19, © Wil Meinderts/Buiten-beeld/Minden; 20, © dougma/flickr; 21, © John Paul Ferrero/Ardea/Animals Animals; 22 (T to B), © duangnapa_b/Shutterstock, © Wollertz/Shutterstock, and © Danolsen/Shutterstock; 23TL, © CPM PHOTO/Shutterstock; 23TR, © KYTan/Shutterstock; 23BL, © Ivan Kuzmin/Shutterstock; 23BR, © NaturalBox/Shutterstock.

Publisher: Kenn Goin
Senior Editor: Joyce Tavolacci
Creative Director: Spencer Brinker
Design: Debrah Kaiser
Photo Researcher: Thomas Persano

Library of Congress Cataloging-in-Publication Data

Names: Giannini, Alex, author.
Title: Coconut crab / by Alex Giannini ; consultant: Darin Collins, DVM Director, Animal Health Programs Woodland Park Zoo Seattle, Washington.
Description: New York, New York : Bearport Publishing Company, Inc., [2018] | Series: Even weirder and cuter | Includes bibliographical references and index.
Identifiers: LCCN 2017034343 (print) | LCCN 2017046093 (ebook) | ISBN 9781684025213 (ebook) | ISBN 9781684024636 (library)
Subjects: LCSH: Coconut crab—Juvenile literature.
Classification: LCC QL444.M33 (ebook) | LCC QL444.M33 G53 2018 (print) | DDC 595.3/8—dc23
LC record available at https://lccn.loc.gov/2017034343

Copyright © 2018 Bearport Publishing Company, Inc. All rights reserved. No part of this publication may be reproduced in whole or in part, stored in any retrieval system, or transmitted in any form or by any means, electronic, mechanical, photocopying, recording, or otherwise, without written permission from the publisher.

For more information, write to Bearport Publishing Company, Inc., 45 West 21st Street, Suite 3B, New York, New York 10010. Printed in the United States of America.

10 9 8 7 6 5 4 3 2 1

Contents

Coconut Crab	4
More Odd Crabs	22
Glossary	23
Index	24
Read More	24
Learn More Online	24
About the Author	24

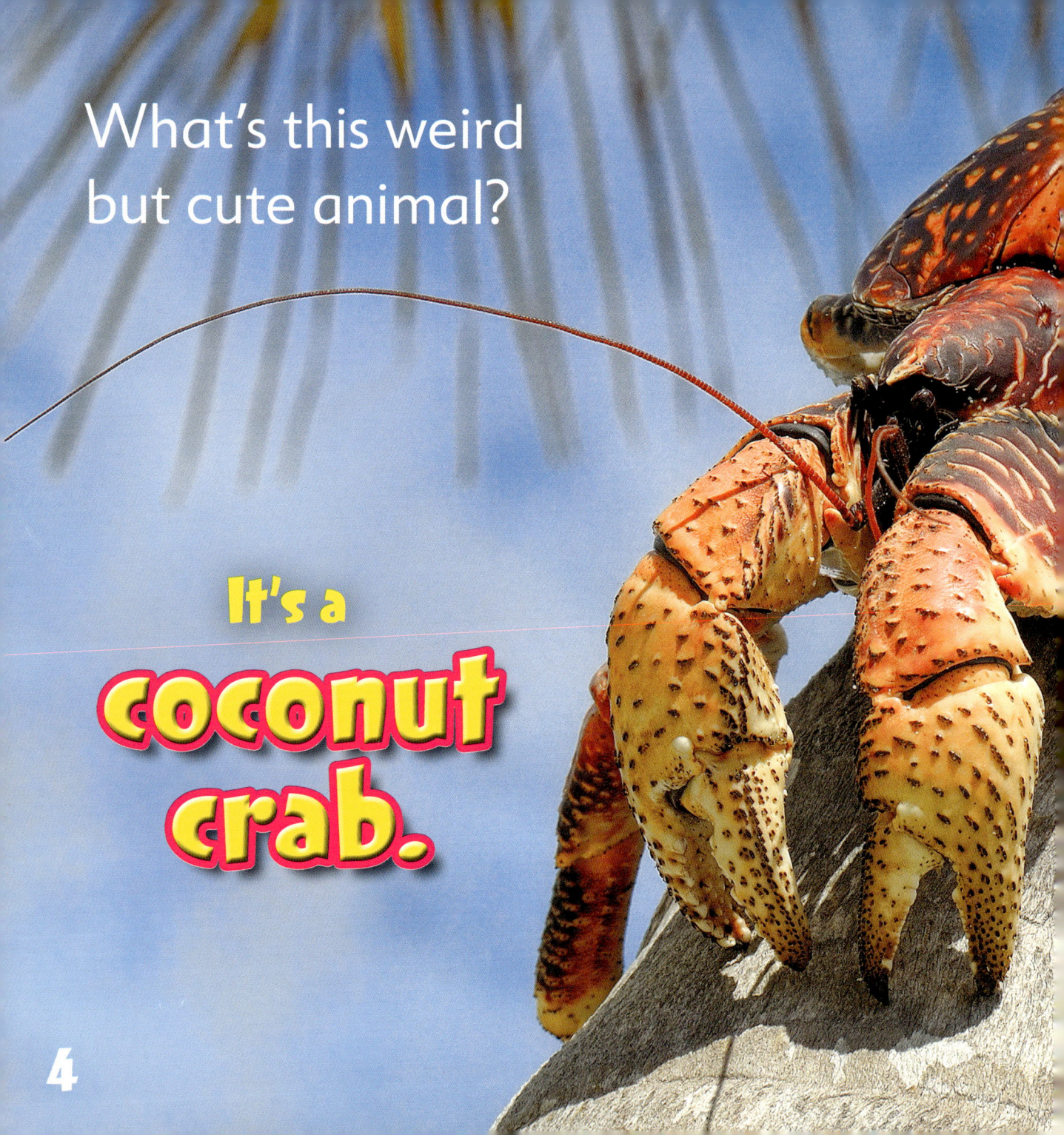

What's this weird but cute animal?

It's a **coconut crab.**

Coconut crabs are the biggest land crabs in the world!

They can grow to be the size of a small cat.

Coconut crabs live on islands in the Pacific and Indian oceans.

When coconut crabs are young, their bodies are small and soft.

How do they stay safe from birds and other enemies?

They crawl inside a coconut shell or seashell for protection!

seagull

Young coconut crabs don't need their shells for long!

coconut shell

Over time, their bodies harden like a suit of **armor**.

They get bigger—and never stop growing!

An adult coconut crab can weigh up to 9 pounds (4 kg).

Coconut crabs have a giant left claw.

Watch out! That huge claw can close as hard as a lion can bite.

The claw can even crack open a coconut.

That's how the crab got its name!

The claws are used for finding and eating food.

Coconut crabs eat fruit, plants, and dead animals. Gross!

dead bird

On some islands, coconut crabs eat rats!

red crab

They also dine on smaller red crabs.

Smell that? A coconut crab can!

These animals have a great sense of smell.

The crabs wave their **antennae** to sniff out and find food.

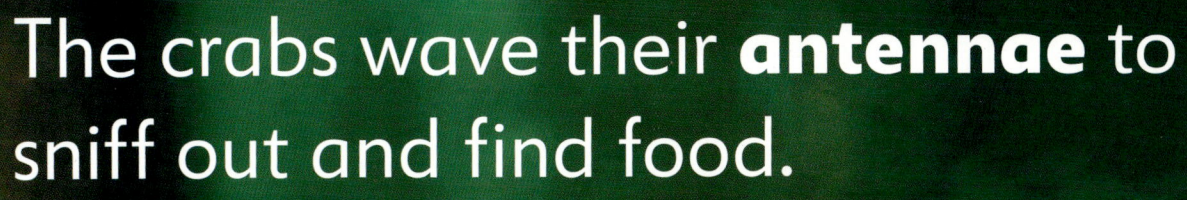

Coconut crabs can smell food from miles away.

While looking for food, these big crabs walk a lot.

They can travel more than 2 miles (3.2 km) every day!

Coconut crabs can also climb tall trees to find a meal.

Coconut crabs have ten legs. Two of the legs are tiny and hard to see.

Coconut crabs are also known as robber crabs. Why?

They steal food from other animals.

Sometimes, they rob shoes, **utensils**, and other things from campsites!

a crab stealing a shoe

More Odd Crabs

Fiddler Crab
Male fiddler crabs have one giant claw. To get a female's attention, the male waves his huge claw in the air like a flag!

Horned Ghost Crab
These tiny crabs are super fast and can run quickly across sand. Some are ghostly white. They also have unusual eyes on long stalks.

Vampire Crab
This cute crab has a creepy name, but don't be afraid! The vampire crab doesn't suck blood, but it does have bright yellow eyes.

Glossary

antennae (an-TEN-ee) the two body parts on an animal's head used for feeling and smelling

armor (AR-mur) a hard covering that protects the body

nocturnal (nok-TUR-nuhl) active at night

utensils (yu-TEN-sulz) kitchen tools such as forks and spoons

Index

claws 5, 12–13, 14, 22
climbing 19
enemies 8
food 14–15, 17, 18–19, 20
shell 5, 8–9, 10
size 6, 10–11
smell 16–17
walking 18

Read More

Lunis, Natalie. *Crawling Crabs (No Backbone! The World of Invertebrates).* New York: Bearport (2008).

Zappa, Marcia. *Coconut Crabs (World's Weirdest Animals).* Minneapolis, MN: Big Buddy Books (2015).

Learn More Online

To learn more about coconut crabs, visit
www.bearportpublishing.com/EvenWeirderAndCuter

About the Author

Alex Giannini is a writer who works in a library. Sometimes, he even writes when he's in the library.